I0456538

Published by Frankenstein Pickles
First published 13 March 2017

www.jojette.com

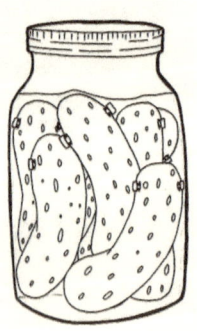

published by
Frankenstein Pickles

For Joshua.
Thank you for putting up with my neverending nonsense.

CHAPTER ONE

Coffee strong enough to wake the dead

You know how when people say their boss is an idiot, it's usually just because their manager or employer has done something recently to piss them off? I mean surely there can't be that many idiots in charge of things right? Yeah well. My boss is an idiot. A bona fide moron. Not just here or there. All the time. I honestly don't know how he got his job. Well actually I do. He owns the company. His only major talent, well talents – I'm feeling generous – are being rich and kissing arse. And he's rode them both to fame and fortune with his Creative Agency, Blahlamo. Well maybe not fame and fortune. But in his mind he's a creative genius. Unfortunately he's also my boss and at the moment it's annoying the shit out of me.

This time though he went to far. Or I was over the nonsense. It's definitely one of the two. And after yet another meeting with our latest million-dollar client, I had finally had enough. Here's the rub. My boss, who can't even open and read an email, continually promises the world but without the budget to deliver it. Then we lose money. Then he gets pissed because we lose money. Then he gets snarky, and yells at the staff for losing money, when it's down to him all along. He gives in to client deadlines we have no hope of meeting, and then expects us all to work nine to midnight everyday to fulfill *his* promises. He on the other hand goes home promptly at six. The bastard. So this client. He promised we could do everything they need within their miniscule budget. Half the shit they want is impossible unless you want to spend millions of dollars in R&D. How the shit are we going to send their customers their own personal hologram via email? What the actual shit? He doesn't know what he's talking about. This is the problem.

As I sat there, in the meeting, staring at my notepad, I realised I had written 'kill Michael Rochard and this could all be over by lunchtime' on every available piece of paper real estate. It was not looking good. Besides I had no available weapons to kill him with, and I didn't want to go to jail for it. Perhaps if I just ignore today it will go away?

The client of course nearly pee'd their pants in excitement. But for me, well I knew what was coming. This afternoon I would pull Michael aside, take him into the conference room and tell him that 90% of his promises to the client were un-achievable. We'd have a barney. Finally I would get him to understand what he had done. He'd be all put out. I'd try and be nice about it. Because *I* am an idiot. Then Michael would ask me to go and speak to the client. Put things right. This would be the catalyst for the torrent of stupidity that would follow on from this interaction and carry over into the rest of the week. That was my week shitting shitted. I was well and truly over it.

As the meeting finished up I realised it actually was lunch-time. I decided to head out and get some air. Let my fury abate with the breeze. It wasn't only my boss who was ruining my day though. My doctor had also had a good hand in shitting up my week. I had gone to see him to get some test results the previous day, and the motherfucker had told me I had the big C.

Cancer. That shitty scumbag of a disease that begins with mutated cells that are found in your own body. It's a potluck kind of disease. Though having a genetic disposition towards developing it adds nicely to the fuckers chances. It's a nasty little bastard. Invading your body. Sometimes you just end up with the C-bomb when there's no family history of it at all. And you're a non-smoker who errs on the healthier side of life... like me. Shitting shit it. Six months I was told. Six short months left. It was pretty advanced. No options. And here I was thinking I was just over worked and run down. That's why I'd gone to have some tests done, and this was the result. I was only 27 years old for Jeff's sake! I shouldn't even have to think about cancer! I hadn't told anyone yet. In hindsight I really should have taken someone to the doctor with me. I never dreamed I'd get this news though. So right now I was the only one who knew about it. I needed to make some plans before I told anyone. I didn't want everyone trying to take over my last few months. Controlling it with their own craziness and emotions. It's my demise damn it. I wanted to live it out on my own terms.

There was a chill in the air as I walked down the street. Headed for my usual place. As I passed the Café La Morte I saw it was for sale again. Funny that. It was up for sale pretty much every six months. I'd never even been in there once in the three years I had worked for Blahlamo. I always passed it off as being some kind of hipster paradise. Something I diligently tried to avoid. Beards and lumberjack nonsense. Boat shoes and oversized glasses. La Morte's tag line was *Coffee strong enough to wake the dead.* I guess it was kind of quaint.

I leaned forward to get a better look in La Morte's window. It actually looked nice inside. Polished wood, brass, leather, green velvet booths. It looked like an old fashioned speakeasy that served coffee. Why had I never even given this place a go? Oh yeah. My own prejudices. Stupid arrogance and stereotypes. That's all. My own hang-ups and worthless opinion. Well today was a good enough day as any to try something new. Cast off the shackles of judgey old judgement. Maybe they had good stuff to eat in there, and I could do with a dead waking coffee right now to be honest.

Pulling open the door I inhaled the wonderfully reviving aroma of fresh coffee and toasted goodness. The place was mostly empty, and so I chose a booth up the back to make my own. No wonder this place was always up for sale if this was the lunchtime crowd. It was hardly at capacity considering it was a prime time of day to be serving food and drinks. The waitress came over to take my order. A pretty girl in a mint dress with a thick black belt. Long red hair cascaded down her back, but it was not natural red. It was bright and artificial. Dyed, obviously. She smiled and asked about my day, her green eyes taking in the details of my face. I said it was good, fine, and ordered coffee and a sandwich. She walked away.

I took off my jacket and laid it on the seat next to me in the booth. It was warm inside the Café La Morte. I stared straight ahead and waited for my coffee. The girl in the mint dress returned shortly, and placed a cup of coffee in front of me. The cup was ornate, made of china, with gold trim. More a tea cup really. For some reason that bothered me.

I took a sip. It was good. Damn good. Hot. Why had I not been here before? Oh that's right. Judgey McGee. The girl in the mint dress returned with my sandwich. Salad. I'm vegetarian. Have been for years. I took a bite and realised I wasn't hungry. I'd been thinking for too long now about what I had coming to me over the next six months. Inoperable they had said. Brain cancer. Who would have thought that. Not me. Ha! But I guess I covered that before right? I have an appointment with the oncologist this afternoon to weigh up my options. Chemo. Radiation. Whatever. It might prolong my life, but the results speak for themselves. Incurable. What would you do?

As I sat in the booth, sipping my coffee, my mind continued to wander. The girl in the mint dress came back. She wanted to know if everything was OK.

'Yes, good, fine,' I said and managed a smile. I asked when the café had gone up for sale.

'Last Tuesday,' she said.

'Last Tuesday, or the Tuesday just gone?'

'Hmmm,' she wasn't sure, but she knew it was a Tuesday. She smiled awkwardly and left.

I touched the green-flocked wallpaper on the walls. It was fuzzy and pleasant. I liked this place. What if I didn't go back to work this afternoon and just stayed here and drank coffee, ate my sandwich, then had dinner and drinks later? Fuck it. I could see the café also had a good stock of alcohol behind the bar... counter... whatever. I didn't have to go back to work. I really didn't have to do anything now. It was a very refreshing thought. And it was nice and warm in here. Quiet. No pressure. No clients. No idiot boss. I could just stay here. I could just stay here forever. Well six months anyway.

Why the fuck not?

I could even buy this place. Sell everything I owned and just stay here until I died. Drinking coffee. Eating sandwiches. Lunching. Dining. Drinking. Meeting people. Fuck yeah! But how to go about it? How did you buy a café? I guess I needed to speak to the owner. Perhaps this was all crazy, but life is short. Especially mine now. I looked over at the girl in the mint dress

9

and called her over.

'I think I'd like to buy this place,' I said.

She laughed. It was a pretty laugh. Like glass tinkling.

'I'm quite serious,' I added.

'OK, mister quite serious, I'll get the owner.'

She left, and came back with a handsome, square-jawed gentleman. Tall and lanky, well dressed, though not fashionably. This man had style. It was clear no one needed to tell him who he was. His greying hair was swept back from his face, in a style not seen since the 1920s and I wondered immediately what he was doing running a café. It didn't seem to fit. He smiled and sat down.

'Now why,' he drawled in an accent I could not place, 'would a nice young man like you want to buy Café La Morte? You don't strike me as the hospitality type.'

'Neither do you,' I smiled up at him, 'but I am still considering it.'

He stuck out his hand with a laugh. His name was Luke, and it was nice to meet me. We talked for hours and worked out a deal. It turned out I was getting more than I bargained for, but if I could stick it out, Luke would see me right. So what does that mean? Well, it turns out Luke is short for Lucifer. That's right, he's the Devil. And he can fix me, de-big-C me, but he had some conditions. Like all contracts, there are clauses. The strangest part is I believed him. Straight up. No horse shit. I had no reason to question him really. Even if what he said wasn't true I had nothing to lose. Well, my life, but that would happen anyway. There was just something about him. Call it a vibe. Call it a feeling. The uncanny way he was able tell me things about myself that not even my family knew. His knowledge of my current medical condition.

I wouldn't call it conclusive evidence. There's no way

any human could have known that shit. It didn't freak me out though. It was reassuring. He knew exactly what I needed. And how to provide it. But it would cost me my last six months on Earth. I didn't care. I'd pretty much decided how I was going to spend the time I had left anyway. Somehow this seemed to fit nicely into Luke's plan, and was reflected in his offer.

So what was the offer? Details. I would buy the café, and all would be well if could stay inside it, 24 hours a day, for my last six months on Earth. I couldn't put more than one foot outside, or the deal would be broken. I would be obliged to eat, sleep, shit, shower, breath in the La Morte. And I couldn't tell anyone why. Or I would be done. That would suck a bit. People are stupid. They always want to know why. If I die before the six months is up, well that's just bad luck.

If I can last six months though, Luke will remove my cancer, and I walk away. What's he getting out of it? I'm not sure. Yet. I think he just likes doing stuff for people. He's gotten a pretty bad rap since the creation of religion, he explained. Why did he have to be the bad guy? He tells me God is a jerk. Well that was the consensus. I'm inclined to believe him. For my part, this was a news flash to me. I'm an atheist. Luke went on to add, none to bitterly, that he never did any of that shit he's been credited with. The snake and the apple, Joan of Arc, Blues musicians, original sin, sin that was perhaps not so original. The list could go on forever. Essentially religious nut bags had tried to pin any evil nonsense on him, and even some stuff that wasn't evil – like acts of nature. Hurricanes, earthquakes, floods, fires, locusts. He wasn't angry, he said.

'Just disappointed.'

I guess it's easier to manipulate people if they have a common enemy. Luke had made a convenient scapegoat. For the last two-thousand years or so he had been laying low. Out of the spotlight. Off the radar. But that didn't stop the accusations. It was hurtful he said.

'Were you ever?' I asked.

'Evil? Yeah, sure. We all were in the beginning, but I got bored of it. I gave it up. The others didn't. Once I dropped out of the life however, I became an outsider. No one wanted to be seen with me. That's what the banishment was all about. That's how I became the convenient one to blame. It's so easy to pin the shit on the voice that doesn't agree with you, call *them* out as evil if they disapprove, and don't want to continue on with something that is so obviously wrong.'

I empathised. Since his exile he had been running La Morte, and similar ventures over the years. Helping people like me where he could. People with some kind of potential. Or so he said. For what, I don't know. Apparently La Morte was the one who determined this. Like all things mythological, it had a mind of it's own. Then, all the chosen had to do was make it through. To the end of their time. And be reborn. Or some shit. I guess Luke had to pass the time somehow. Being immortal would kind of suck. It must get boring after all.

A casual glance at my watch told me we had been talking for two hours. I had finally relaxed. I didn't give a crap that my boss would be expecting me back for our three o'clock meeting with our next million-dollar client.

The first catch of my new business venture was that I couldn't leave La Morte as of the moment I signed the contract. So I knew I would have to sign it before I changed my mind. I would have to figure out how to quit my job, sell my flat, and get my possessions dropped off at the café, and all without telling my parents, family and friends what was really going on.

I could foresee this causing issues. But I would cross that bridge etcetera etcetera...

Reaching into a pocket on the inside of his jacket, Luke pulled out a sheaf of folded paper. Obviously the contract of sale for the Café. Handing it over to me with a beautiful green fountain pen, he smiled expectantly. I must confess I didn't read it through. As I said I was scared I would change my mind. Taking the pen I scribbled my scrawly signature across the dotted line. As I watched the ink dry I watched my old life drift away like embers on the wind. Cool to touch. Ashes.

CHAPTER TWO

Take this job

Luke smiled as I handed him the signed contract, and signalled for the girl in the mint dress to come on over. He introduced us. Her name was Erica. She would help me tie up any loose ends I needed to in order to move myself into one of the rooms above the café. I could live up there as technically I wouldn't be leaving the café. That made it all easier. I could have visitors, and the situation would seem a whole lot more normal. Or less weird? I didn't know which yet. Luke explained that Erica was in a similar situation to myself, well similar in that she had the same desired outcome of not dying. Or rather not being dead in her case. She also lived in the rooms upstairs, but her story was a bit more complex. She was nine months in to a 12 month stint as her death was a harder mystery to solve. Apparently she had gotten into some trouble, or perhaps it was an attempted suicide? I didn't want to pry. A drug overdose was involved. She had been missing, was still missing. Her family were looking for her. Luke had found her slumped in the doorway of La Morte one morning. He had picked her up and taken her inside. Suspended her impending death and made her a deal. She would do 12 months in the café and then she could go back to her family. Her life. Back too normal. She didn't mind. In fact she was enjoying her time at La Morte. Coffee strong enough to wake the dead, she smiled. The only thing she missed was company. Real company. Not just customers. Luke was away a lot so he didn't count, she smiled awkwardly this time, and Luke laughed. He agreed. She missed her family. Her friends. Her cat, Arnold, whom she was sure her mother would have taken in. After all she had always threatened to take the cat home with her.

Luke smiled knowingly as Erica walked off. She returned a few moments later. In her hand was an old, black telephone. It had a brass dial, with ornate numbers in the little holes.

'Make your calls,' he said, as he stood up to leave.

'Oh ... but I have my mobile...' I trailed off.

'It might not work all the time in here, reception is terrible,' smiled Luke, turning away.

Weird. I watched Luke head out the door into the sunlight, before turning to the phone. First call was to my boss. Get the easiest one out of the way. I was quitting. He could do nothing about that. Selling my flat and organising the move would be more involved. Sherry, the receptionist, answered on the third ring. I told her to ask Michael to meet me at La Morte. I wasn't going anywhere. Then I told her what the deal was. She said she would have him here in five minutes. I hung up the phone and smiled. I could wait that long before I started on anything else.

Erica brought me a glass of water.

'Well don't you look like the cat that got the cream? I think this change might be good for you,' she observed, smiling.

'I'm quitting my job,' I explained.

'Sounds like you would have quit it sooner or later judging by that smile on your dial.'

'Yeah, it was the pits. My boss is on his way over here now.'

'Oh, in that case can I get you anything?'

15

'No, I think I want to make this quick and painful,' I smiled.

'You got it,' she laughed.

Erica left me to it. Swishing off in that mint dress of hers. A few minutes later the door opened. In walked Michael. He looked pissed. Or tired. Or maybe even happy? I could never tell with this guy. It took his eyes a moment to adjust to the light. Or lack of it in this dusky place. Then he spotted me. He smiled slightly and headed over. Taking a seat opposite me in the booth, he signalled for service. He was always like this. Impatient, demanding, looking for solutions before weighing up his options. The menu was right in front of him. He didn't even glance at it. Straight to ordering. He was perfect management material. If your want your manager to be a dick, that is.

'So, you wanted to see me here?' he asked as Erica wandered over, 'coffee black, and a muffin, blueberry and white chocolate please,' he said to her without looking up.

'Sure,' said Erica walking off again. Vaguely I wondered how far she walked in a day. Around the café.

'Yes,' I said simply, 'thanks for coming down, I couldn't be bothered coming back to the office to be honest. I quit,' I said with satisfaction.

Michael looked at me and went through the usual emotions. Shock, denial, anger, acceptance.

'Fine, how much notice are you giving?' he asked stonily.

'I'm owed 6 weeks leave,' I replied, 'take that as my notice, but I'm not coming back to the office, I'm done.'

'I can't accept that, you need to ...'

'No I don't,' I interrupted him, 'I don't have to do anything for you, what I am suggesting is perfectly legal, you can't deny my leave and you can't force me to go back to the office, I'm done.'

'Well this really sucks,' he said, looking down at his hands, 'you're really leaving me in a spot here, if you're looking for something else, I wouldn't expect me to give you a good reference.'

I couldn't resist sticking the knife in now. I knew what I was about to say I hadn't planned to share with him. But it was too good an opportunity to pass up. I wanted the bastard to feel bad.

'I'm dying Michael. I have cancer,' I said, and watched his face fall. Fuck him.

'Oh, ah... sorry,' he said. I watched him squirm awkwardly in his chair.

'And I don't think threatening to give me a shit reference is going to help me at this point.'

'I'm sorry, I didn't mean that, really, I was just angry you're leaving.'

'You're a shit boss, Michael.'

'Oh well... yes... I guess I deserve that. Don't worry, I'll sort out your pay and your bonus,' he added.

A bonus huh? Guilt money. I wasn't owed a bonus. But whatever. I'll take it.

'Thank you.'

He got up to leave just as Erica returned with his coffee and muffin, ready to take away. He nodded curtly to her and pulled out his wallet.

'It's on me,' I said looking up at Michael, who continued to look awkward. It was no longer satisfying. I wanted him to leave. It was just sad now. He seemed to sense this.

'Better get back to the office,' he said, 'all the best.'

'Sure.'

'Do you mind if I tell the office why you're leaving?'

I thought about this. I realised that as soon as Michael started spreading the word I would start loosing control of my personal information. Word would get around fast. It was my own fault for being sadistic.

'Not yet please,' I settled on. That way I could control the dissemination of my information. I hoped. I sighed. I knew Michael would probably tell them anyway. If only to save his own ego. It would not do to have his staff leaving because he was terrible.

'Sure,' he answered. I knew he was lying.

'Good-bye Michael,' I sighed as he turned and walked away.

CHAPTER THREE

Tying up loose ends

One down. A few to go. The job was done, sorted. Next up I had to get rid of my apartment. Thankfully it was not uncommon for people to meet Estate Agents in cafes. I picked up the phone. Held it for a moment. Put it back in its cradle. I knew no Estate Agents. I needed the Internet. Did the café even have it? Why the frack didn't I check! How could I live here without the Internet for six months? I frowned. Scratched my head. Rapped the table. How was I going to do this? Once gain Erica to the rescue. She must have been watching me. My frown for all to see. She wandered over and smiling and placed an iPad in front of me. The devil's own distraction.

'We have free wi-fi,' she said simply, smiling and wandering back to the counter.

OK. Let's do this. I hooked up meetings with a few places. Let them convince me they were the best to sell my little flat. Now what? Moving stuff? Calling the parental unit? Brother? Friends? I didn't want to talk to anyone. I knew it would be a hassle. But it had to be done. You can't run from emotional situations forever. Best to get it over and done with.

First I called my parents. They agreed to meet me at the café the following morning. Concern obvious in their voices as I spoke to each in turn on the phone. I still couldn't tell them anything of substance of course. That was part of the deal. But I gave them enough to think this was a sound decision. It would become more difficult later on. Next I called my brother and my best mate. They agreed to help me move my stuff. I could tell they thought I had gone a bit Howard Hughes when I told them I couldn't help them. Oh well. Let them think what they want. In six months this would all be over. And by this time in two days I would have all my stuff with me. In the mean time they had agreed to drop over a few necessities. They also wanted to check out my new mad scheme. They'd be here in a few hours. I could handle that.

In the mean time I needed a drink and some information from Erica. I look up at her cleaning glasses behind the counter. Everything went a bit fuzzy for a moment. Like it wasn't real. Perhaps my brain wasn't coping. Too much change for one day. Erica caught my eye, grabbed a bottle and two glasses and came over. Sliding into the seat opposite me, she opened the bottle and poured two large measures. Whisky. Japanese. Nice.

'So, you wanted to ask me about some things?' she said.

'How did you know?'

'That look, quizzical, but not knowing how to start the conversation. I've seen it before.'

'Just how long have you been here?' I asked, suddenly alarmed.

'You know how long, Luke told you.'

'Oh yeah....' I drifted off.

'Look, not everyone makes it. Luke asks a lot. Have you ever spent months locked inside, unable to leave? I was a drug addict, I'm used to not seeing sunlight for days on end. I can handle it. Anything that doesn't involve being high is a win for me. Others, well, they're a bit more mentally fragile. The minute you go out that door before your time is up and,' she slapped her hands together, 'it ends! You're done before you have a chance to live again, literally.'

'I get it,' I said pensively.

'Yes, well, since I've been here I've seen three hopefuls come through. The last only fell through a few weeks ago. It's difficult because you get to know people. Like them. Form friendships. Then you watch them throw it all away for one breath of fresh air. Maybe they think it's worth it. But I have to see their faces before they go. I see the regret, the despair. I don't want to go through it again, so I will answer any questions you have, and I will help anyway I can. For the next three months, anyway,' she smiled.

'Oh that's right, you only have three months to go, you must be excited to get back to your life.'

'Yes and no, but anyway shoot.'

'OK, so you're stuck here same as me right?'

'Yep.'

'So who does all the ordering, food supplies, liquor that sort of thing?'

'Luke takes care of everything. Bills, supplies, everything. You just have to run the place. He'll take the cost of everything out of the profits. I mean you can run that side yourself if you like but if he's gonna do it for you I don't see why you would want to.'

Hmmm. Why indeed. I was willing to play along on this side of it. I wasn't into doing admin. If Luke wanted that responsibility. He could have it.

'And you're happy here?' I continued with my questions.

'As happy as I can be. It was difficult at first, but as soon as I made peace with the building it all went smoothly.'

'Wait... what?'

'I'm sure Luke mentioned the Café La Morte has a mind of it's own right?'

'Yes, he did in passing, I didn't think anything of it.'

'Well the building is possessed.... You know haunted... by a number of ... souls I guess you'd call them. Mostly they're a good bunch but there's a few nasties. That's why the other hopefuls didn't make it. La Morte drove them mad, but it took a little more than that to push them out the door. You really have to be tough to stick it out.'

Ah-ha! I thought. There's always a catch. Oh well. I should have read the fine print, but I was sure I could handle it if Erica could.

'So how did you make peace with La Morte?'

'I offered them a sacrifice. The other hopefuls. It's a bit difficult to understand but as far as I am aware, if someone leaves before they've served their term the café gets their life force, or something, it keeps it going, it needs the energy.'

'Well that's charming I must say,' I was quite affronted. She better not try to pull that shit on me.

'Look, it's survival of the fittest right? La Morte was giving me a really tough time, and I had to do something. So I bargained three souls for safe passage through my 12 months. You being number four, you're quite safe from any of my deals, but don't judge me yet. You still have to get through your first week, let alone six months. I'm guessing if you're smart, you'll need to make your own bargain.'

Suddenly I didn't feel like talking any more. I said as much and sulked into my corner. Erica sighed and went back to work. Perhaps when I'd calmed down we could pick this up again. I needed to know more about this damned Café I'd signed my life away for. And I needed to stop judging her.

CHAPTER FOUR

Word gets around

By the time I stopped feeling sorry for myself it was getting dark outside. Erica was getting ready for the dinner and bar crowd that surely would be showing up some time soon. I was ready for a drink myself. Getting up slowly I wandered over to the bar, and sat myself down on one of the stools lined up under the counter.

'Back with us then eh grumpy?' smiled Erica.

'How long is your shift?'

'Well we don't open until 10, and I work until 8, so 10 hours. I don't mind. It's not like I have anywhere to go.'

'So we close at 8?'

'No, no, sometimes Luke comes in and keeps the bar open, we get an interesting clientele here, you'll see.'

'And if Luke doesn't come in?'

'You're the barman now sweetheart, you can't sit round lunching all day, you have to do something or *you will* go mad.'

'I've always fancied myself as a barman,' I laughed, lightening up and feeling my mood lift finally.

'Let me get you a drink, what do fancy?'

'Thanks Erica, I'll have a .... What will I have? There's so much choice!' I exclaimed looking behind the bar at the seemingly endless shelves filled with wondrous bottles of booze.

'I'll pick something nice for you,' she said as she

swished away. I noticed she had changed into something a bit more suited for the evening.

'What do you do when your shift finishes?'

'Oh I have plenty to do, sometimes I stay for a drink, sometimes I read, but I'm also finishing off my degree by correspondence, so that keeps me busy.'

'What are you studying?'

'You'll laugh at me, I'm not saying.'

'Oh come on!'

'I want to be a Physicist,' she answered simply.

'Wow, that's impressive... why did you think I would laugh?'

'Oh most people see me waitressing or working behind a bar and they assume I'm stupid, or that I couldn't possibly be smart enough to pass.'

'Well that is ridiculous!'

The conversation paused naturally as we fell into an awkward silence. Erica brought me my drink. It was a delicious amber colour. In the light it sparkled with gold flecks. Turning my head on it's side I studied Erica closely.

'Thank you.... Erica... did you really send those others to their deaths?'

She sighed audibly as she turned around. A serious frown creasing her forehead.

'I had too. You'll see what it's like.'

'Perhaps the La Morte will be nice to me?'

'Perhaps, there's always a first time,' she smiled doubtfully.

'But what did you do?' I asked, but before she could answer Luke suddenly appeared in the doorway, smiling like a demon and looking pleased with himself. He had a duffle bag under one arm and his other arm was wrapped around the shoulders of my brother Tim. My best mate, Sarah was following close behind. She looked worried. Tim on the other hand was obviously impressed by Luke's character. He was a charismatic son of a bitch. I was sure he could win over an ice giant with his charm. If he wanted to. And ice giants existed. Outside Marvel.

Taking a sip of my drink, I was momentarily distracted by how good it was. The perfect gold-leaf whisky. Standing up, I left my drink at the bar and approached the oncoming trio. Sarah stepped forward and hugged me. She looked intently into my face. Her blue eyes searching for madness. A hint of insanity perhaps. Tim slapped me on the shoulder and smiled awkwardly.

'Welcome to my new... to Café La Morte,' I said to slice through the slience.

'It is a lovely café, but why have...' Sarah began.

Luke cut her off. 'Why don't we all sit down and have a drink eh?' he smiled widely. Deflecting the conversation like a pro.

We took a seat in the booth I had been sitting in earlier. Down the back. Near the bar. Erica came over with a bottle of wine and four glasses. Red. Crystal. I was sure it would be excellent. I was right. My brother took a sip of his wine and sat there looking amiable. That was him all over. A wonderful big galute. Sarah ignored her wine and looked into my face again, always searching.

'So, brother, you're a small business owner now eh?' Tim laughed, 'what gives? Bad day at work?'

'You could say that,' I replied awkwardly. My brother could be anything if not perceptive.

'Damian?' pressed Sarah. She was not going to let this one go.

'Look, yes. It was partly due to work. I just wanted a change. I've been in a rut – surely you know that.'

'Yes, but I didn't expect this kind of stark contrast, and in such an unexpected direction.'

25

'Well the deal is done, and I am going to make a go of it.'

'I'm happy for you Damian, I'm just worried.'

'Spoken like a true friend,' added Luke smiling his damnedest and pouring more wine for everyone, 'look,' he added, 'I've said to Damian to give it a six-month trial. In six months if he's not happy with it, then I'll buy the café back, you can't get fairer than that.'

Luke really was a crafty bastard.

'Having second thoughts eh?' smirked my brother, 'it must be a good place then Dames, if he wants it back already.'

I watched Luke out of the corner of my eye over the next few hours. He looked like a king surveying his subjects. Covering all bases, holding off questions, steering the conversation where he wanted it to go.

CHAPTER FIVE

Settling in

My brother and Sarah had stayed until just after 8 o'clock. At which point Erica finished her shift, and Luke took up residence behind the bar. The traffic picked up around 9. Every booth was full. Others were chatting at smaller tables. I had to pinch myself to remind myself that I was actually here. Doing this. That this place was actually a successful bar. How had I never noticed it? I guessed I usually went home from work. Straight from the agency to my front door. I rarely went out anymore. Too tired. Now I knew why. I hadn't ever been past this place at night. Never realised it had a decent crowd. I looked around at the people. Something started to dawn on me. They were all slightly amiss. Just small things. One woman's eyes were all white, with just a black pupil showing. Another guy had weird, purple coloured hands. Well they looked purple. I saw a couple who were almost see-through. Like ghosts. Another man was crooked from head to toe. I smiled into my wine. There was always a catch. I figured all these people had been through the Café at one time or another ... or Luke had something to do with them in some way. Perhaps made them that way? Before I could dwell on this burgeoning conspiracy theory any further, Erica appeared on the opposite side of my booth. I realised I hadn't really moved all afternoon.

'So you noticed I guess? They're all... a bit strange?'

'Yes,' I said simply.

'They're not all Luke's former ... he didn't do this if that's what you're thinking, some of them are just genuinely lost people. They feel welcome here.'

'Oh.'

'Like Luke himself, you know, rejected by the mainstream, or simply too self-conscious to even try to fit in, the uncool, the odd, the different.'

'But there are some former owners of the cafe here too?'

'Oh yes, but they may not talk to you so be tactful OK?'

'I never said I was going to talk to them,' I responded indignantly.

'Yeah well, I'd bet money on you thinking about it, anyway, I'm off to study, plus your'e parents will be here in the morning so don't stay up too late. You'll need to be on tomorrow in case they have any curly questions. Night!' she smiled, getting to her feet and skipping off through the 'Staff Only' door that led out the back, to the living quarters.

It was at this point I realised I didn't know where my room was, or anything else about the rest of the building. I finished my wine in a gulp, instantly grimacing at what a mistake that was. I grabbed the bag of clothes my brother had bought me and took off after Erica.

'Night Damian!' called Luke from the bar as I scooted past, 'I'll lock up OK?'

'Thanks Luke!' I called, as I continued on my way, catching Erica at the bottom of some stairs.

'Hey!' I called, a little out of breath, 'I just realised I have no idea what's back here and where I sleep, can you show me?'

'Sure, of course,' she laughed.

We started with downstairs. First up the lounge

room. It was not at all what I was expecting. The was an open fireplace to the left, surrounded by three large chesterfield sofas. In between the sofas was a long oak coffee table. To the right of the fireplace was what I recognized as a globe bar. I'd always wanted one. It was currently open revealing a half dozen bottles of fine looking liquor, and (what I assumed) were crystal glasses. To the left of the fireplace was a further small sitting area centred around a TV. On the far wall was a floor to ceiling library, and to the right of that was a door leading to what I would soon see was a chef-spec kitchen.

Walking through to the kitchen, Erica explained Luke would make sure the fridge was stocked with whatever I needed. I simply had to give him a list of what I wanted. Convenient, but it meant again I was reliant on Luke for something else. Heading back to the stairs, we walked up the steep flight of steps. The upstairs comprised the whole space of the Café downstairs, and the back area we had just come from. There was a bathroom to the far right of the stairs, which was a grotesque example of luxuriousness. Claw foot bath tub, with a cabinet full of powders, soaks and bubbles to match. Frosted glass shower and shelves full of fluffy towels piled up to the ceiling. I guessed that either Erica or Luke had a penchant for primping.

Finally we got to the most important part of the house. Our own space. Four bedrooms led off from the hall, each with it's own fireplace for heating. Erica explained that her room was on the right, next to the bathroom, and so I could take whichever of the others I wanted. All the rooms locked with a key. Erica then disappeared into her room leaving me feeling like a fool for a moment standing in the hallway. Sighing to myself, I moved into action, choosing a room to the left and opening the door. Taking it all in. The room was amazing! I could not have hoped for a better place to make my home for the duration. The room appeared huge inside, and I had to do a double take. To my right was a four poster bed with velvet curtains. Who doesn't love velvet. Then to the left was a small lounge area of my very own, complete with small open fireplace, and mantle. In front of that were two black leather chesterfield chairs and a small mahogany coffee table. To the left again was another floor to ceiling book shelf, which I would discover was filled with works by my favourite authors. To the right of the fireplace was a dark wood buffet, filled with whisky, and inside a cupboard was a small fridge filled with fruit, mixers, soft cheese. It was as though the room had been set up just for me. It was perfect.

Dumping my bag on the bed I wandered over to the fireplace and got it crackling. The room was chilly. I shivered into my jacket. Perhaps I should have a shower and get changed. It had been such a long day and my parents would be arriving in the morning. Best to get an early night.

Walking down the hall to the bathroom, I took in the walls of the hallway. Though they were covered in intricate flocked wallpaper, they seemed naked. I guess I was just used to seeing paintings hanging everywhere, like I had at home. Shutting the bathroom door behind me, I showered quickly and then put on some tracksuit pants and a loose t-shirt, then wrapped myself in a terry robe. I loved that robe. It was ridiculously warm and comfortable. Throwing my wet towel in a hamper, I turned to the door and shuffled back to my room, and the roaring fire that was now heating the high-ceiling space. Grabbing a book from the shelf, I sat in a chair and peeled back the first page. I had no idea what time I fell asleep, but

I was awoken by an awful scratching sound at my door some time before the dawn. My neck felt like someone had gaffer taped it into the most awkward position possible. Never sleep in a chair. Sitting up I rubbed my neck back into shape, and looked sceptically at the door. Was there some kind of animal out there? Was La Morte seeing if it could fuck with me already? At that point in time I didn't care. Too tired.

'Thanks for waking me! I would have slept in the chair all night!' I said to the room, getting up grumpily and stalking over to my bed. Then I saw it coming through the door. A river of rats. But not real rats. Ghost rats I guess you would call them. They were all kind of transparent and writhing. Sniffing and clawing. I thought they were cute. Rats wouldn't scare me. Let alone ghost rats. I didn't believe in ghosts. For all I knew I was still sleeping. Having a bad dream.

'Nice try,' I added sarcastically, to no one in particular, before getting into the bed and rolling over onto my side. Ignoring the ghost rats I fell almost instantly into a deep sleep.

CHAPTER SIX

A visit from the parentals

I awoke in the morning to find the fire had long since burned itself out and there was a chill in the air. Running my hand across my forehead I vaguely remembered the events of the night before but wrote it off as a bad, wine induced dream. Throwing back the covers I got up and pulled on a robe. Looking at the time I realised my parents would be knocking on the door within the next half hour and I needed a coffee. I hoped that the kitchen downstairs didn't have some complicated coffee machine. A kettle would do.

Trudging to the bathroom, I passed a mirror on the wall, catching sight of myself briefly. Something didn't look right. In fact something looked very wrong. I stopped in my tracks and backed up. I was almost scared to look up as it was dawning on me what the problem was. Why I could only really see out of one eye. I had assumed it was just sleep sticking the lashes together, and that a splash of water would fix it. But no. Slowly I looked up at myself. My stomach turned. I felt faint. One of my eyeballs was hanging by its optic nerve, out of its socket. Rubbing against my cheek. Resisting the urge to vomit, I sat down hard on the cold floor for a moment. I would have to figure this out. Perhaps I was still dreaming? That would make sense! I pinched myself hard on the leg. Ow! OK. Not asleep then. Shit. How did this happen? Then I recalled the rats from the night before, though I didn't think they would have done this. Logic dictated that they would have just eaten the eyeball. Or at least 'ghost licked' it. OK what then? It had to be something in La Morte that had done this. I needed Erica. I also needed to sort this out before my parents arrived. I only hoped that my eye wasn't damaged. A little dry perhaps, but not damaged.

'Ericaaa!' I called at the top of my voice. She responded immediately, as though she had been expecting something. Her bedroom door flew open and she appeared fully dressed and with a first aid kit in hand. Yep, she knew what was coming all right.

As she got closer to me I could see all the colour drain from her face. I don't think she was quite expecting something so dramatic after my first night here.

'Oh, oh no, what has she done to you Damian!'

'Ummm ... this?' I said, pointing at my dangling eyeball.

'I'm not sure I can help with this. This is beyond me. I thought bruises, cuts, she usually starts simple, but she's gone all out with you.'

'So it would seem,' I murmured, 'can we call a doctor?'

'I don't know, I don't see why not, that's not breaking the rules, but they'll want to take you to hospital, and ask questions you won't really want to answer...'

'Yes... yes good point.... What would you do?'

'I ... don't know... you're taking this very well though.'

'Well there's not much I can do about it now, so no point in getting upset.'

'I see... aren't your parents going to be here soon?'

'Yep... Okay.... Let me think for a second,' I said slowly, then thinking out loud, 'what if I just pushed it back in?'

'What! No! I don't think that's a good idea!' shouted Erica, alarmed.

'Why not? I can't die in here, I'm under Luke's protection aren't I?' I reasoned, 'he doesn't want me to die in here, or get too fucked up, the game is to get me to go outside, so logically I should just be able to push my eye back in, as long as I'm careful, and use some gloves and saline.'

'Are you serious?'

'Very, look what have I got to lose? If it doesn't work I'll call a doctor OK?'

'If you're sure... well, I can't stop you.'

'I have to try! Now pass me that first aid kit, I'll go in the bathroom so you don't have to watch,' I said grabbing the kit and stalking off, while Erica stood in the hallway dumbfounded.

Once in the bathroom I placed the first aid kit on the sink, and closed the door behind me. I washed my hands. Opened the kit. Pulled on a set of surgical gloves and popped a vile of saline open. Dousing my eyeball and cavity first. As the cold saline hit my eye I shivered. I was really going to do this. Alright then. No fear. Looking in the mirror I pushed aside the nausea that threatened to topple me from consciousness. Reaching up gently I touched my eyeball. I felt instant revulsion. It was soft. Gelatinous. Gross. With my other hand I peeled back my eye lid and without stopping to think popped my eyeball back in. I felt it slurp back into place and promptly fainted. When I came to I found myself lying on the cold tiles, a folded towel under my head. Erica was beside me. Looking concerned and wiping my forehead with a cold, damp cloth.

'Oh thank goodness! I thought I'd lost you! I heard the thump and dashed in here to find you in a crumpled heap on the floor. It looks like your eye is back in place though. Can you see out of it?'

Slowly I opened my left eye. To my surprise I could

see fine. It had worked.

'Looks like your theory about this house and Luke might be right,' said Erica sadly, 'I wish I had been smart enough to figure it out before I...'

'Nevermind. It's got nothing to do with smarts, I was half guessing and got lucky, how long have I got until my parents get here?'

'I reckon 15 minutes. Enough time for a quick shower and some wake-up juice, I'll meet you downstairs in 10,' said Erica, helping me to my feet and then walking off.

She was right. This was no time to dwell on the morning's incidents. I could do that later. For now I had the parental unit to deal with. Not wasting time to go to my room and grab clothes I simply jumped in the shower. I could grab some jeans and a t-shirt on my way downstairs in a few minutes. Turning on the water I let the heat and steam clear my mind. I washed my face gently. It was still tender, but I could live with it. I was sure it would start to bruise up slowly, and hoped Erica might be able to help me out with some concealer. A bit of a cover up never hurt anyone.

10 minutes later I was downstairs, sipping at a cup of coffee and waiting patiently for my parents. Erica kindly brought over a toasted sandwich, and as I took a bite the door clicked open. The parentals had arrived. I could only hope I would fool them, and that they would go away quickly. As horrible as that sounds, I didn't want to worry them. The longer they stayed, the more chance I had of slipping up.

CHAPTER SEVEN

Two night's down

My parents left some time after 2pm. I was left to my one devices for the moment as Erica served customers. Luke had also taken off. Things to do. He had dropped past to meet my parents and assist their transition, as he called it. I didn't know whether to feel thankful or slightly creeped out. Luke was taking what felt like an overly curious interest in my life.

Taking a spot in what I decided would be my favorite booth, I looked over at Erica, who nodded and brought me over a glass of wine and the paper. Looking at me for what felt like the longest time, she finally spoke.

'Yep, I certainly did a good job covering up the bruising on that eye. You're very lucky it's so dark in here. I might get you some ice though, that eye is still pretty swollen.'

'Thanks,' I managed a smile, 'it still feels a bit tender, but hey I can see out of it so visibility for the win!'

'You're a goof!' laughed Erica, spinning off back towards the room to follow up with her customers.

I turned to my wine and took a sip. I then picked up the ice-pack that had suddenly appeared on the table and held it to my poor face. What a day. But I was about to be interrupted from my self-musing.

'Do you mind if I sit here? I know there are other tables, but I do love it sit in a booth,' said a wonderfully, raspy voice. How could I say no to a voice like that.

'Sure,' I nodded.

I looked up to see a woman at least 40 years older than myself, with a bit of a Lauren Bacall air about her. Her silver hair was set in a style not really seen since the 1950s. She was dressed in an outrageous purple suit, with her manicured nails a vile, evil shade of green. Her face was perfectly made-up. She looked like a movie star. She placed her bag on the leather bench seat, and slid herself in beside it.

'I used to come here with my husband,' she said, but way of explanation.

'Oh,' I said.

'Yes, for many years, it hasn't changed much. My husband passed away a few years ago. Since then I come here every year on his birthday and have a glass of wine.'

'Oh,' I said again, 'I'm sorry for your loss. Please let me buy you a glass.'

'That's very kind,' she smiled, and so our conversation began. Her name was Rosalie, and we talked on into the evening, when Luke finally returned. He recognized Rosalie immediately, greeting her with a kiss on the cheek and then strolling off towards the bar. I guess he was working tonight, which meant Erica would finish shortly. I wondered if she would want to watch a movie or something?

Promptly at seven, Rosalie stood to leave. She hadn't expected to be there all day, she said, but it had been a lovely time. Evidently much nicer than the time I was in for later that night.

Erica was too tired to watch a movie. Fair enough considering the hours she worked. So I stayed up by myself, lying in bed, watching *Nightmare on Elm Street*. I have no idea what made me choose that particular film. I drifted off to sleep about half way through as the fire in my room began to die out. When

I woke, it was not pleasantly. I was secured to the bed. Four limbs to four corners. Floating above me was an absolute horror. I was frozen in terror. Either side of the bed were more. I couldn't say what they were. Ghosts? Specters? Boogeyman? Or just plain old monsters. And yet as I lay there, drenched in a cold sweat and almost unable to breathe, I noticed something odd about the visions before me. They all had Freddy Krueger's face. Now either I was having a very bad dream, or there were really several ghosts of Freddy Krueger who had decided to tie me up and hang out in my bedroom. Immediately I relaxed. This had to be La Morte at work. Or at least some of her residents. They would have seen me watching the movie of course. I'm sure they thought they were being scary or hilarious. Or both. But to me it seemed rather pointless.

'Bravo,' I said sarcastically, 'did you really think I wouldn't recognise one of the most recognisable faces in horror?'

The shapes shimmered uncomfortably for a moment.

'Now,' I continued, 'if you know what's good for you, untie me and let me get back to sleep. I had better also find all my faculties intact by the morning.'

The apparitions shuddered more violently this time.

'I don't care if you don't like it. I've figured you out, La Morte out, and if you don't leave me the fuck alone I am going to start hurting all of you. Tomorrow,' I said calmly. I was now fully awake and fully pissed off.

The apparitions shuddered again and vanished. I wasn't sure if it was because they believed me or because I wouldn't be any fun to them if I wasn't scared. Suddenly my arms and legs were released. Pulling the blankets over me I rolled over onto my side and touched my face. Everything was where it should be. I slowly felt over the rest of my body. My wrists and ankles were obviously sore. So was my stomach.

But I was too exhausted to do anything about it now. I'd have a look in the morning.

CHAPTER EIGHT

I'm definitely not a morning person

I woke in the morning in terrible pain. The adrenaline of the previous night had worn off. Every cell of my body wanted to double over, but that only made the pain worse. There was definitely something wrong with my belly. Pulling back the covers I found they had stuck to me in the middle of the night. Dried blood was everywhere. What the hell had happened to me! I tried to sit up, but was too weak to move. Once again I would need to rely on Erica for help. Calling out at the top of my lungs, I winced in pain again as the effort proved too much. I passed out. When I came too Erica was next to me on the bed.

'Bloody hell! What happened to you?' she exclaimed as she walked through the door.

'Oh you know just the usual night.... horror movies, bit too much wine, open fire, sleep... Freddy Krueger,' I smiled back.

'Well it looks like you tried to sacrifice yourself to the Gods.'

'Really? What the fuck happened to me?'

'Well for a start you have some weird symbols carved into your stomach.'

'Right,' I replied.

'Aside from that you have an awful lot of bruising.'

'Thanks a lot Freddys,' I mumbled.

'I would say it has all the hallmarks of La Morte.'

'Yes,' I agreed, 'and I know just how to stop it.'

'OK, how?' she seemed skeptical.

'I'm going to hang some paintings.'

'Oh, right, what? Wait, but Luke told me...,' she said.

'I don't care what Luke said, I only know La Morte will not like it one bit.'

'Fine,' she sighed, giving up on trying to speak to me in this condition, 'well then my dear curator, I think we better clean you up first?'

'Yes, yes please,' I smiled to myself. In my mind I was all ready to fight fire with an atom bomb.

Erica wrenched open a big black medical bag that had been sitting next to her on the bed. I looked at it dubiously, but what choice did I have but to trust her. As she started pulling bits and pieces out of it, I was actually surprised. Not only did she have pain killers, but local anesthetic and everything she needed to stitch me up. She seemed to have done this before. Perhaps she had? But I would have to leave my questions for another time.

'You're a mess,' she said again injecting me with the local.

'Yes,' I agreed, wincing.

Erica sighed.

'I need hot water and towels. I have to get rid of this dried blood, so I can see what I am doing. I don't know why the house is being so rough on you, I certainly never experienced anything so ... destructive,' she said getting up slowly and walking out the door towards what I assumed was the bathroom.

'OK?' I called out to her as she left.

'I'm serious!' she exclaimed on her return, arms laden with towels, disinfectant and a bowl of hot water. Pulling on some surgical gloves she prodded my side gently.

'Can you feel that?'

41

'Thankfully no.'

'OK, I'll get started, but let me know the minute you feel pain OK? After I'm done I'll leave you some pain meds and let you get some rest.'

'Thank you,' I said again, I mean what else was there to say?

'Look, I've been here 9 months,' Erica said suddenly, her brow creasing as she worked, 'and I've seen many .... attacks by the house in my time, but I have never seen her ever be as severe as she has been with you... so who are you?'

'I'm literally no one, but I guess this means she ... it must fear me for some reason. It's the only explanation. It wants me out of here bad.'

'You're starting to scare me a bit.'

'Look, don't worry. You'll see. By the time I'm finished this house and I will be best friends,' I said with a confidence that came from I know not where.

CHAPTER NINE

Everyone has a weakness

I slept late through the morning. Waking only when the pain killers wore off. Erica was checking in on me every hour or so. I wasn't worried. Just angry. And La Morte was going to pay.

Rummaging through my bag I pulled out a small tool kit that I had asked my brother to bring over with my essentials. Taking out a hammer and a few nails, I was decided it was time to start making a few modifications to my room. Even if it was against our "tenants agreement".

In between visits to my bedside, Erica found me about to strike the first nail.

'Wait!' she cried out, a look of concern creasing her brow.

'Why?' I asked with all the innocence I could muster.

'Well... I....'

'Exactly,' I said, 'this house has attacked me and now it's time for a taste of my own medicine.'

'But Luke said...'

'Yes?'

'We're not supposed to modify the house.'

'Oh yes, and I know why too. I've been thinking about this since late yesterday, when I was talking to Rosalie. I've got to try something. I can't go six months without sleep and with ever increasing injuries!'

'Ok, well I know nothing about this then,' smiled Erica walking off. At least I knew she understood.

I turned back to the task at hand. Holding a nice big nail against the wall with my left hand, I had the hammer poised to strike in my right. Taking a deep breath, I drew my arm back, and gave the nail a good hearty blow. It drove straight into the wall with a soggy kind of thud. It was sickening. A moment later a trickle of blood slithered down the wallpaper. I had been right. If La Morte didn't play ball tonight, I would hang every piece of artwrok I could get my hands on, one nail at a time. Smiling to myself I wiped the blood away with my finger and walked off. The rest of my belongings would be here on the weekend, including a wonderfully large collection of framed pictures. And now I had somewhere to hang them.

Walking back to my room, I caught sight of my face in the hall mirror. I almost felt bad for a second. I looked like a madman. Sadism was not second nature to me. Normally. This was not a side of myself I wanted to nurture. A sharp pain in my belly brought me crashing back to my senses. Fuck La Morte! Look what she'd done to me! I would have these scars forever now. No, I was doing the right thing. This wouldn't happen again. Taking some more pain meds I trundled myself back off to bed. I'd need a few days of bed rest at least to get over this one. Luckily I hadn't needed stitches. Getting into bed slowly so as not to re-open my wounds I drifted off to sleep almost immediately, sleeping though until the next morning. La Morte had left me alone. I think it got the message. Well, I hoped. Can a building rationalise? I didn't know. I thought I had better add a stern verbal threat for good measure. Looking up at the ceiling I was so busy writing my speech in my head that I didn't even notice I had fallen asleep again...

CHAPTER TEN

Why you little...

Well it turns out La Morte is really fucking stupid for a building. I had four weeks of blissful, undisturbed slumber and then last night the bitch broke the truce. I was now sitting here nursing a broken left hand. It should have been my right, but then again it might have been my neck. I can't complain too much. I thought the old girl had gotten the message. I'm not to be trifled with. I guess she thought she was clever. Breaking my hand. Thinking I couldn't do her any more damage with my hammer and nails. Ha! I would walk over a bed of hot coals if I thought it would make this damned place leave me alone for good. I'm not even 2 months into my stay yet. I'm not putting up with any more crap. Today a doctor is coming to set my hand. I've told them I'm agoraphobic. Can't go outside. So they'll come to me. Luckily. Anyway. At least I can still go to the toilet by myself. I'm not risking anything happening tonight though. Three weeks ago my brother dropped off all the artwork I own. As soon as the doctor has gone I'm going to hang me some pictures.

The doctor was 15 minutes late. Not too bad really considering. He met us out the back of the café and looked me up and down. I'm sure I seem pale and sickly. Thankfully I can blame this on the pain. Sitting down across from me he examined my hand, while his nurse got everything else ready.

'Yep, definitely broken, good call there,' he smiled.

'Yeah I figured when I couldn't move the fingers....'

'This won't take long. I'm just going to give you something local for the pain and then we can sort this out. Are you sure you don't want an X-ray first?'

'Can you do that here?'

'No,' he lamented, 'I wish I could but the law would kill me.'

I like him. He does things outside the box. Hence I'm not being dragged screaming out the door. To a hospital. Where I probably should be.

'I appreciate you coming out to do this though.'

'Don't thank me until you heal straight, otherwise you will have to come into hospital and they'll have to break and re-set your hand.'

I shuddered. Fuck that.

'I'm sure it will be fine. I'm a good healer,' I smiled weakly.

'Can I get you a drink, anyone?' piped up Erica, popping her head around the door.

'No thank you,' replied the doctor and nurse as one.

'So, what happened here?' asked the doctor.

'Had a bit of a fall,' I lied, obviously.

'Yes, I can see the stairs there, had a few too many?' he smiled awkwardly.

'Uh... yeah sure.'

'Well just sit tight, I'll be done soon,' he added, getting to work finally. Dipping his head he concentrated on my hand. Doing his best to get it right.

'He likes to focus,' said the nurse out of nowhere.

About 20 minutes later he'd finished setting my hand. Removing his gloves he handed me a bottle of prescription painkillers.

'The cast will take about 30 minutes to set, so just sit tight for a while, and then you can start moving around. Call me if you have any issues, but you should be fully healed in about six weeks.'

'Thank you doctor .... oh, how do I pay for this?' I asked. I knew I had forgotten something important.

'Don't worry about that, Luke will take care of it,' said the doctor, looking up suddenly as Luke chose that minute to walk in.

'Hello Jim... well, what do we have here?' he asked the doctor.

'This young man fell down the stairs, and earned himslef a broken hand,' said the doctor, obviously uncomfortable. I wondered how they might have known each other.

'You need to be more careful, Damian,' said Luke smiling. I knew he knew what was going on. Somehow I think the doctor did to.

'Well, I better be going,' said the doctor getting up too quickly and stumbling slightly. The nurse now looked uncomfortable too.

'Yes, it was good to see you Jim,' said Luke, his voice a low rumble. I shivered. The doctor started back involuntarily.

'Thanks doc,' I said, sticking out my right hand. The doctor looked at it but didn't take it. I moved my hand back to my side. Awkward.

'I'll show them out,' said Erica, trying to lighten the mood, but it was a bit too late for that now.

'No need,' smiled the doctor, gathering his things quickly. Moments later he and the nurse were out the door.

I looked down at my hand in its cast. I could barely pinch my thumb and forefinger together, but it would be enough to hold a nail. I smiled to myself.

'You're in good spirits,' said Luke. He had no idea.

'No use crying over a broken hand,' I said, 'plus the doctor gave me some pretty strong pain killers.'

'OK, back to bed you,' said Erica interrupting firmly.

Obviously she didn't like where this chat was going.

'No, no more sleep. I want to stay up. I'm going to watch some TV down here... it's safer,' I looked up at Luke, raising one eyebrow.

'Do you need anything from the store? I'm going,' he said, conveniently changing the subject. I guess he could also feel the heat rising from me as I grew more agitated by the second.

Good. I wanted him out of the way. I needed some space for what I had in mind, I didn't want Luke here to stop me.

I waited about an hour. My cast had dried and Luke had finally gotten moving after taking his sweet time having coffee and reading the paper. Almost as soon as he left I jumped up and raced upstairs. Grabbing a sheet from the linen closet I piled on a bunch of framed paintings and photos, folding the sheet over them so I could carry a whole bunch at once. I thought I felt the room shudder as I worked. Perhaps she knew what was coming, but nothing happened. It was also possible she had no power during the day. I smiled devilishly to myself as I picked up the hammer and a bunch of nails and put them in a pillow case. I was ready. But where to start? I figured the hallway outside our bedrooms would be as good a place as any.

Walking over to the end of the hall, dragging my stash of artwork behind me, I started planning how to hang my art. I didn't want this to look like a mish-mash-hash job. I wanted it to look good. Opening the sheet I took the pictures out one by one and walked the length of the hall, placing artwork on the floor as I went to mark the positions I wanted to hang them. I started a separate pile for the works I wanted to hang in my room and downstairs. I might have to save those in case La Morte tried to get funny with me in the future. It also depended on how generous I was feeling when I had finished with this lot.

Once all my artworks were in place I returned for my nails. Taking a bunch and holding them between my lips, I picked out a good one, placed it on the wall and hit it with all my might. A devastating scream ripped through my head. I felt it more than heard it. Of course La Morte couldn't draw attention to herself to the public. I had a feeling she was calling for Luke to come and protect her. I needed to work fast. Not stopping to hang the pictures yet, I continued along down the wall. At each incision the nail had made in the wall, a trickle of blood flowed. I kept working.

After I finished the hall I headed for my room. Fuck it. I would keep plugging in nails until Luke came back. But he never came. La Morte screamed and screamed, but he left her to my wrath. Perhaps he knew. She had been giving me such a rough time, perhaps he felt it was justice. I moved down the stairs, taking more nails. I had enough large pieces left to make a decent impact on the lounge room there. I finished up with my nails and returned upstairs. I savored my task as one by one I hung each piece, knowing the weight of the frame would add a little extra pain.

I had nearly finished when Luke returned. Looking up at me from the bottom of the stairs, he seemed neither angry or ... well I had no idea how else he would feel. I walked slowly down the stairs, meeting him at the bottom.

'Been busy I see?'

'Yep.'

'OK, I think it's time we had a chat,' he said, turning on his heel and heading back into the café.

CHAPTER ELEVEN

That's the way it's gonna be

Luke sat down across from me in my favourite booth. Erica had given us both a small glass of scotch and then made herself scarce. Smart girl that Erica. Across from me Luke stared at the table top, gathering his thoughts or perhaps just wanting to avoid looking at me right now. I could feel the disappointment emanating from his every pore. Before he said anything, I thought I would nip this in the bud.

'Look, before you say...'

Luke cut me off.

'What were you thinking?' he said calmly. It was actually quite intimidating.

'I think you know what I was thinking,' I replied grimly.

'Hmph, well I guess this is my fault. I hadn't actually told you not to ... make any ... changes to the building.'

'Oh Erica told me,' I leaned forward, smiling like a madman.

'She did? And you just went on and did that anyway?'

'Yep.'

'And you think this isn't going to have repercussions?'

'Oh I know it will, but I don't care – I'm not going through this shit again!' I yelled, getting to my feet and lifting up my shirt to reveal my scarred torso. I also managed to scare half the café, who I could feel jump in fear.

'Take it easy there Damian, sit back down,' said Luke calmly, but I had seen the alarm in his eyes. Things were going my way now.

'Look, La Morte knows now that I am not to be fucked with. If she tries anything else, next time I'll take a chainsaw to the bannisters,' I growled.

'Where are you getting a chainsaw?' smirked Luke, but he looked a little surprised.

'Ever heard of online shopping? They deliver right to your door, anything you want.'

Luke looked at me in silence for a few minutes. There was no way I was saying anything more. I could do this all day. All day for four more months if I had to. I smiled to myself. I couldn't help it.

'You think this is funny?'

I gave him nothing.

'OK, well I think you've made your point. Given the damage you've done here today I would be surprised if she messes with you again,' he said, gesturing to the walls, 'but she might be even angrier. If she is, I can't help you.'

'You couldn't help me anyway!' I said, holding up my broken hand in defiance.

'Yes well...'

'Well nothing Luke, I own this place, at least for the next few months. I'll remodel the whole thing if I damn well feel like it. If La Morte fucks with me again, I'll burn it to the ground and live in the ashes until my time is up!'

'I guess you could...' he trailed off. I had the system beat and he knew it. For the next few months I'd be happy camping, then it'd be no more cancer, and back to reality.

'You know I could.'

'Right well, I'll leave you to it then,' he said slowly, getting up and walking to the door. He hadn't even touched his scotch, so I grabbed it with my good hand and downed it in one shot.

'Another!' I shouted happily, slamming the glass down on the table, 'and drinks for everyone, on me!' I added.

A cheer went up throughout the café. Erica laughed, and got busy with the drinks. I looked over at her and smiled. I think I had just fallen in love with the prettiest red head in town.

CHAPTER TWELVE

So long and good-bye

I was three months in to my spell at La Morte. Sleeping like a baby. No more hellish night visits from violent apparitions. La Morte was behaving herself wonderfully. I guess she didn't count on my insanity outmatching her own. However today I woke with a sense of dread. I had been worrying on the approach of this day more and more since the sudden realisation that I had feelings for Erica. Today was her last day at La Morte. After this she was free to go. Back to her family. Back to her cat. Back to her old life. I didn't even know if she knew how I felt. How did she feel about me? Did she give a shit? I had been trying to work up the courage to tell her for weeks. I love you. So simple. So mushy. So scary. So much fall out if it goes wrong. Fall out for me. I'm sure she would just walk away and never look back. I would. If I was her. And it was me. I really am just an insecure mess when it comes down to it.

I woke early for once and went down into the deserted café. I wanted Erica's last day to be special. I brewed coffee and set to work making her pancakes. Breakfast in bed. Everyone likes that don't they? Then I would tell her. Then I would only have to face one full day of rejection if... perhaps I would tell her later. As I was making a second batch of batter (my first had been a lumpy mess not fit to serve a rat) Erica drifted down the stairs. She looked refreshed. But also slightly sad. I guess after 12 months you do get used to a certain way of doing things.

'So.... your last day eh? Pancakes?' I asked, smiling my most dazzling morning smile.

'Oh that's so sweet of you, yes thank you, and coffee if it's going please Damian,' she smiled back. I thought I would split at how happy that smile made me.

I poured her coffee and took over a stack of misshapen pancakes. Cream, strawberries, maple syrup, butter, lemon, sugar. I had prepared everything.

'This is quite luxurious I must say,' she laughed. Damn it! Why did I love that laugh so much.

'Now you have to wait until midnight don't you? Before you can head out the door?' I asked. I genuinely hadn't even thought about this. Of course a day ticks over at midnight, so it would make sense.

'Nope, I can go anytime I like. Technically my time was up at midnight last night, so I was gonna pack my things after breakfast and head out. I wanna see my mum and my cat first,' she replied, still smiling widely.

'Are you going to call your mum before your see her?'

'I thought about it. I think I might have to be a bit careful how I do this. I'm going to go to the police station first and hand myself in. I'm still a missing person, and it will be easier for my mum to handle my return if it comes from the police. I think,' she furrowed her brow and looked down.

'Well,' I forced a smile of my own, 'it sounds like you have a plan, and everything is under control, now eat your pancakes before they get cold.'

A few hours later and Erica was all packed. Luke was supposed to come past and say goodbye, but he had yet to make an appearance. Erica wanted to wait for him, to say thank-you, but I suggested just dropping past another time to see him. It was also a good way for me to see her again too. I remember the time being emblazoned on my memory. 3:17pm. She was walking out of my life. Perhaps forever. And there was nothing I could do about it. I still didn't have the courage to say anything. Coward. I watched her walk away towards the door. Open the door. Step out into the patchy sunlight and then immediately collapse in a heap on the cold concrete footpath outside.

My eyes widened as adrenaline coursed through me. I ran through the café, pushing people aside, tearing open the door and within moments I had her cradled in my arms. Serendipitously Luke chose those moment to appear. It felt as though he had planned this.

'What's happened?' has asked innocently, though in my eyes he was anything but blameless.

'She just walked out the door and then... this,' I said not bothering to look up at him.

'Hmmmm,' mused Luke, 'that's a shame.'

'And I guess I've fucked up too now. I've gone outside, broken the rules. Just like you wanted. I bet you planned this all along, you evil bastard!' I screamed.

'Me? No of course not. It looks like Erica just got the date wrong that's all.'

'So, she's gone then?' I looked up at him finally, tears burning my eyes as hatred seared my soul.

'Dead? Yes, it looks that way, but I'll let this one slide for you, after all you were only trying to do the right thing.'

'No mate, forget it, I'm done here,' I said stonily.

'What do you mean?' asked Luke, with more than a touch of surprise.

'I'm out, if she's dead, I'm done too. I don't want to recover. Cancer can kick my arse all over town, I don't care anymore.'

'Look come on, we need to get the girl inside, people are starting to gather,' said Luke, and now I could hear tension creeping into his voice.

'I don't care!' I yelled, laying Erica gently down and getting to my feet. I was beyond angry now. Satan had stolen my girl and I was not ..... well I didn't know what, but I wasn't gonna be quiet about it.

'Damian please....'

'You killed her, you toyed with her for a year and now you've killed her... again... I know it was you who gave her the dirty shot, you think you're so bloody clever don't you? Manipulating all the poor little humans, but I've figured you out, you lying bastard!'

'Well, I am Lucifer...' he began, trying to make light of the situation.

'Shut your mouth before I shut it for you. I researched you, in this mortal form you are fucked,' I said stepping forward and producing a switchblade from my back pocket, where I had been keeping it for days. The long, thin blade shot out from it's spring loaded clip, and before Luke could move I sliced him every which way from Sunday. Blood gushed and poured, covering Luke, me, Erica, the sidewalk. Everywhere. Luke started laughing. Someone screamed.

'Oh Damian you truly are your father's child aren't you, so you love this girl then? There's no other explanation for such completely over the top insanity. I love it!'

'What do you mean?'

'Hang on a moment,' he said, waving his hand elaborately across the sky. In that second time stopped, or at least appeared to.

'What the fuck now?'

'We need some privacy,' he said, 'you've managed to create quite a scene here. We also need to clean up this mess,' he added as he looked up at the clouds. In an instant they gathered darkly together, and rain began to pour, soaking everyone and everything still frozen in time.

'So I haven't hurt you then?' I sighed, realisation punching me in the guts.

'Only ruined my shirt I'm afraid, now come on let's get her inside.'

The minute we entered the café, Erica drew in a sharp breath, returning to life and gasping for air.

'What happened?' she asked, before looking down at herself. Seeing so much blood on herself, along with the blood on Luke and I was too much for her. She passed out. But at least I knew she would be OK for now. Her breathing had evened out, it was almost as though she was...

'Asleep, she'll need her clothes changed before she wakes. I trust you can do that in a gentlemanly way?'

'Yes,' I said sullenly, 'so what now?'

'OK well for a start let me apologise, this was a genuine mistake, I didn't know you were in love with the girl.'

'Moving right along,' I said, my cheeks flushing crimson, 'what do you mean I'm like my father? My father is a fucking accountant for fucks sake!'

'Um no, he's .... Well, look you were adopted right?'

'No, my parents are my parents!'

'Oh right she must have... how can I put this delicately.'

'Put what delicately?'

'You're mother is your mother, her name is Elizabeth right?'

'Yes...' I said, not liking where I felt this was going.

'But the person you know as your father is not really your father.... your father is really .... me.'

Now it was my turn too black out. And fair enough too, I thought as I crumpled in a heap on the floor.

CHAPTER THIRTEEN

It was almost never going to work anyway

When I came to, Erica and Luke were leaning over me. Apparently I had hit my head pretty bad. While I had been unconscious Luke had cleared the café, and so now it was just us three. I looked at Erica again, happy she was alive, but knowing that she had left La Morte too early, so if she ever stepped out that door now she would instantly cease to live. She was trapped. A prisoner. Perhaps this was how Luke operated. He tricked people into leaving early and stole their souls. This way he never had to 'pay out'. I found it so hard to reconcile. Not that Luke was so conniving. He was the Devil after all. That I should have expected. No, I couldn't believe I had been sucked into all this mess. So ready was I to avoid dealing with my problems that I took the first easy path offered to me. And now I was trapped as well. Luke knew I had feelings for Erica and I felt certain he would play on this scenario for his own ends. I was screwed pretty much.

'Welcome back to reality,' smiled Erica, helping Luke lift me to my feet and sit me in a booth.

'Are you OK now, Erica?' asked Luke, concern creasing his brow in a way I hadn't seen before.

'Yes, yes but we can talk about me in a minute, let's sort this one out first, I'll go get changed,' she smiled sadly, walking off towards the back.

'Can you bring back some towels, water and whisky please?' called Luke after her.

Luke sat down across from me and looked into my eyes. Slowly it dawned on me what he had said to make me fall and hit my head in the first place.

'So,' I said shakily, 'you're my father then?'

'As far as I can tell, yes, though your mother never has nor ever would admit it to you.'

'And that's also why she didn't show any recognition of you when she came in a few months ago?' I said skeptically.

'Yes, that's right,' Luke sighed, 'and she hasn't been back in to visit you since then has she? Oh, she calls you of course, but she hasn't actually come in here?'

Sitting in stunned silence I realised he was right. She hadn't been in since then, and I hadn't noticed. What sort of people were we!

'She doesn't want to see me,' said Luke, 'I ah.... hurt her .... No, no! Not in the way you're thinking. Her feelings. I'm not a monster!' he added quickly, noting the anger spreading across my face.

'Can you prove it? Or is this another game?' I asked.

'I can if that is required.'

'I think you probably should,' I insisted.

'OK, fine... fine,' he sighed, 'Erica sweetheart, can you bring me the emerald box too please?' he added calling out loudly.

I didn't like this. Proof would make this real. Real would make this horrible. Proof would make my whole life change. Again. I wasn't really ready.

Erica returned finally and sat down next to me. She poured us each a glass of whisky, and then wiped and bandaged my head. It really wasn't as bad as it looked, she said, still smiling that same sad smile. She then handed Luke the emerald box, which was about the size of a small lunchbox. Setting it gently in front of him on the table top, Luke opened it up. It was filled with folded paper. And envelopes. And photos. Pulling the whole pile out, he handed the stack of papers over to me. Including what looked like a birth certificate, sitting conveniently on the top. It was my birth certificate.

Oh fuck it...

Still silent I shuffled through the letters and photos. There was my mum and Luke at a movie theatre. My mum and Luke on a boat ride. My mum and Luke outside our old house. Wait. What?

'You're older than you think. So is your mother. Your father adopted you when you were still little, and promised your mother he would never treat you as anyone but his own son, never say anything to you. The reason you have no memory of me was quite deliberate. I removed myself from your mind, at your mother's request. It was the least I could do. I owed her that much.'

'So how old am I then?'

'Oh, in human years you may be closer to one hundred and thirty? We do age so very slowly.'

'A hundred and thirty!' I shouted, incredulous. This was just bloody ridiculous! I felt Erica jump a little in her seat, looking at me alarmed. A hundred and thirty?!

'Your adopted father really is a very good man, Damian.'

'So what did you do to my mother?' I asked angrily. I had no other emotional place to go right now. Anger felt right.

'She wanted a human life, she could have lived forever but she didn't want to. I wouldn't follow her. I felt it was too boring, too normal. I have missed her, every day, but she is not the woman I knew. She got what she wanted. One life. Her own life.'

'So she was once immortal?'

'Yes, we were together for a long time, I didn't want to leave her but I also didn't want to watch her grow old and die. Then she met your father, and well ... I faded into the background.'

'How old is she then?'

'Hmmm, let's see... by now she would be four hundred and six? Though the human aging process has caught up with her.'

'So, what does this mean for me? Am I immortal or human, or a mix of both? Can I choose?'

'Yes, no, no and ... yes.'

'Right and I guess that my cancer?'

'Is already taken care of, would have healed anyway, eventually, but I wasn't sure if you were who I thought you were, however after your response to La Morte ...'

'What do you mean?'

'Well it was so fast, so clever... so brutal...'

'So?'

'Well no one else had ever thought to do that... plus I kinda asked your mother anyway.'

'That probably explains why she hasn't come back then,' I said sarcastically.

'Might have had something to do with it.'

'So I'm cured then? Can I leave this place now?'

'Why? Don't you want to stay here ... at least finish up...'

'Well I don't need to, if I'm cured, but what about Erica?'

'Oh yes, well she never finished her stay,' he said awkwardly.

'I don't want her to die, I love her damn it!' I said angrily, before the shock of what I had just done hit me. I am such an idiot! There she was looking at me. Not comprehending what was going on. Maybe she hadn't been paying attention. That would be a relief to be honest.

'Damian! That's so sweet but why?' she asked looking at me in all innocence. She had been paying attention. Blast.

'I don't know – why does anyone love anyone? Hormones?' I replied weakly. I wanted to crawl into a hole and die. I wished Luke would stop time again. Perhaps just freeze Erica this time and I could run far away.

Taking hold of my hand Erica shook her head softly and smiled.

'I would have liked to take advantage of that, too bad I'll be dead soon,' she said.

It broke the weirdness of the situation beautifully. No idea why. It just worked. Why did she have to be so wonderful!

'No you won't,' I said finally, 'I have a feeling Luke is going to sort this out for us right now. Perhaps I just need something to bargain for?' I added hopefully.

Luke smiled. We were back on familiar territory.

'Damian, I wouldn't let her die knowing that you love her. I'm the good guy remember? Not a monster? That's the truth, whatever you might think of me. I've got a bad reputation, but it's all based on lies. Now as for a deal, here's what I can do for you...'

***

Later that night as Erica and I sat having a cuddle on the couch, watching *Deadpool*, I thought back over the afternoon's events. Luke's solution had been a clever one, and I hadn't really lost that much in the end. Half my life for Erica's. That's what he had done. Given her half of my life. So we weren't quite immortal, but we wouldn't live forever either. A good balance. We would have to keep running La Morte however, and work with whatever charity cases Luke sent our way as he carried on much as he had before, but it was a fair enough deal. Surprisingly. I suppose Luke wasn't that bad after all. At least Erica and I could both go outside now. See the world. We could enjoy our lives together. And I would have time to get to know Luke. I didn't think I would ever call him dad, but he seemed all right. And he was a blood relation after all. I could let him be part of my life, I guess he had saved it for me anyway.

www.ingramcontent.com/pod-product-compliance
Lightning Source LLC
Chambersburg PA
CBHW020600130626
46552CB00007B/2966